HERGÉ

THE ADVENTURES OF TINTIN

CIGARS OF THE PHARAOH

LITTLE, BROWN AND COMPANY

BOSTON/NEW YORK/TORONTO/LONDON

70019965

$ 9.95

Translated by Leslie Lonsdale-Cooper
and Michael Turner

The TINTIN books are published in the following languages :

Afrikaans :		HUMAN & ROUSSEAU, Cape Town.
Arabic :		DAR AL-MAAREF, Cairo.
Basque :		MENSAJERO, Bilbao.
Brazilian :		DISTRIBUIDORA RECORD, Rio de Janeiro.
Breton :		CASTERMAN, Paris.
Catalan :		JUVENTUD, Barcelona.
Chinese :		EPOCH, Taipei.
Danish :		CARLSEN IF, Copenhagen.
Dutch :		CASTERMAN, Dronten.
English :	U.K. :	METHUEN CHILDREN'S BOOKS, London.
	Australia :	REED PUBLISHING AUSTRALIA, Melbourne.
	Canada :	REED PUBLISHING CANADA, Toronto.
	New Zealand :	REED PUBLISHING NEW ZEALAND, Auckland.
	Republic of South Africa :	STRUIK BOOK DISTRIBUTORS, Johannesburg.
	Singapore :	REED PUBLISHING ASIA, Singapore.
	Spain :	EDICIONES DEL PRADO, Madrid.
	Portugal :	EDICIONES DEL PRADO, Madrid.
	U.S.A.	LITTLE BROWN, Boston.
Esperanto :		CASTERMAN, Paris.
Finnish :		OTAVA, Helsinki.
French :		CASTERMAN, Paris-Tournai.
	Spain :	EDICIONES DEL PRADO, Madrid.
	Portugal :	EDICIONES DEL PRADO, Madrid.
Galician :		JUVENTUD, Barcelona.
German :		CARLSEN, Reinbek-Hamburg.
Greek :		ANGLO-HELLENIC, Athens.
Icelandic :		FJÖLVI, Reykjavik.
Indonesian :		INDIRA, Jakarta.
Iranian :		MODERN PRINTING HOUSE, Teheran.
Italian :		GANDUS, Genoa.
Japanese :		FUKUINKAN SHOTEN, Tokyo.
Korean :		UNIVERSAL PUBLICATIONS, Seoul.
Malay :		SHARIKAT UNITED, Pulau Pinang.
Norwegian :		SEMIC, Oslo.
Picard :		CASTERMAN, Paris.
Portuguese :		CENTRO DO LIVRO BRASILEIRO, Lisboa.
Provençal :		CASTERMAN, Paris.
Spanish :		JUVENTUD, Barcelona.
	Argentina :	JUVENTUD ARGENTINA, Buenos Aires.
	Mexico :	MARIN, Mexico.
	Peru :	DISTR. DE LIBROS DEL PACIFICO, Lima.
Serbo-Croatian :		DECJE NOVINE, Gornji Milanovac.
Swedish :		CARLSEN IF, Stockholm.
Welsh :		GWASG Y DREF WEN, Cardiff.

Artwork © 1955 by Casterman, Paris and Tournai.
Library of Congress Catalogue Card Number Afo 19681
© renewed 1983 by Casterman
Library of Congress catalogue Card Number R 159731
Translation Text © 1971 by Methuen & Co., Ltd., London
American Edition © 1975 by Little, Brown and Company (Inc.), Boston

Library of Congress catalog card no. 74-21620

20 19 18

Published pursuant to agreement with Casterman, Paris
Not for sale in the British Commonwealth

Printed in Belgium by Casterman Printers s.a., Tournai

CIGARS
OF THE
PHARAOH

This is the life, Snowy. A really quiet holiday for a change...

A holiday, indeed! I'd call it a deadly bore.

We'll be arriving in Port Said tomorrow. We go ashore for the day.

Our next stop will be Istanbul. We'll go ashore there too.

I'd settle for Marlinspike.

PORT-SAÏD

ASIE

SHANGHAI

HONG-KONG

ADEN

BOMBAY

COLOMBO

SINGAPOUR

Piraeus, Naples, Marseilles, then home through the Straits of Gibraltar.

How about that for a marvellous cruise, eh, Snowy?

Marvellous...You mean dull as ditchwater!... Why doesn't someone fall overboard to brighten things up?

Stop!... Stop!... HELP!

! ?

Excuse me, but what are you doing?

Surely you can see: I'm rowing.

But you're not in the water!

Nor I am! What an observant young man you are!

Now I wonder why I was rowing...

To rescue your papyrus, I expect. It blew overboard...

My papyrus?... My priceless manuscript?... Overboard?... Nonsense! I have it here.

But... I saw a paper blow into the sea!

What were we chasing, then?

Oh, yes... I remember now; it was just a travel brochure. You don't really think I'd let go of this do you?... My magnificent papyrus... the key to the lost tomb of the Pharaoh Kih-Oskh. Scores of Egyptologists have tried to find the spot...

Every single one has vanished! But I, Sophocles Sarcophagus, shall be the first to reveal this wonder to the world.

I hope you will... But tell me, what's that queer symbol?

I don't know. I think it's the royal cipher of Kih-Oskh. But if you are interested, why not join me tomorrow in Port Said. We'll go on to Cairo, and find the place shown on my papyrus.

Good idea!

Till tomorrow then. Goodbye, young man.

What a strange fellow!

I beg your pardon, captain.

You clumsy nitwit! Can't you look where you're going?

So sorry, I mistook you for a ventilator...

Imbecile!

3

You?... Arrest me? You must be joking!

Joking? When we open one of these drawers you'll see what sort of a joke this is!

There! Someone tipped us the wink, and how right they were! Narcotics! That's heroin!

Next morning...

Who could have planted drugs in my cabin?

Someone who wanted me out of the way... But why?

Smells fishy!

Here we are in Port Said. Just a cable's length from the quay... and here I am, locked in the hold!

Hello... they're beginning to disembark... I wonder...

Come on, come on ... drift a little bit closer...

I ... er... could you possibly take us ashore?

A few minutes later...

Here we are, Snowy... in Port Said.

Well, well! What a pleasant surprise!

Happy New Year!

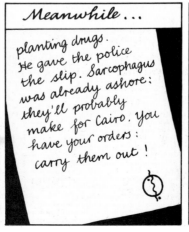

Meanwhile ...

planting drugs. He gave the police the slip. Sarcophagus was already ashore: they'll probably make for Cairo. You have your orders: carry them out!

He won't get far, if my name's Thompson!

To be precise: if my name's Thomson we won't get far!

Later, somewhere near Cairo...

According to the papyrus the tomb can't be far away...

And soon...

You wait for us here. We will return this evening.

Yes, effendi!

You see, a discovery of this importance must be kept absolutely secret.

Yes, of course.

You seem to know the area very well.

I don't know it at all; the papyrus gives very detailed instructions.

We're getting very close now...

You have a remarkable sense of direction!

If the information is right, we shall find the tomb of Kih-Oskh at this very spot...

What did I tell you! The tomb! I've found it! O noble Pharaoh, I have come!

Fame at last! The name of Sophocles Sarcophagus will live for ever!

WOOAH WOOAH

Hello, what does Snowy want?

A cigar... A cigar out here... How peculiar.

Good heavens! That's extraordinary! The Pharaoh's emblem on the band!

FLOR
FINA

I wonder what Doctor Sarcophagus will make of that ...

Hey!... What in the...? He's gone!

I say, Tintin, it's just like the band of the cigar!

Where in the world can he have gone?

Yooee! Doctor Sarcophagus! Yooee!

Not a sign! He's completely disappeared ... What was that he said? "Scores of Egyptologists have tried to find the tomb ... Every single one has vanished!"

I smell danger: there's dirty work somewhere round here ...

Wooah! Wooah!

Hello... what's up?

Aha! That explains it! Doctor Sarcophagus went inside: we'll just have to follow him ...

Down that dark hole? ...Brrr...

Come on, Snowy, careful now...

THUD

You heard that, Snowy? We're trapped in the tomb!

8

Yes, they're absolutely identical with the one I picked up outside...

I wonder if the answer to all this lies hidden inside these cigars... I think I'd better take a look...

What...what's happening?... My head... I feel ...

That smell... some sort of drug... someone's trying ...

No! Not that!!

Meanwhile...

The bearded master told me to wait...When they did not return at nightfall I called loudly, I shouted...They did not answer me ...

The next night...

Good. 'Sereno' is at the rendezvous. Unload the camels.

I'll flash the signal.

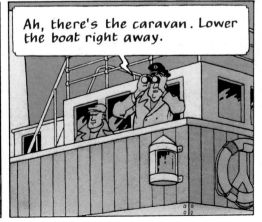
Ah, there's the caravan. Lower the boat right away.

If there's nothing else to catch in this bit of sea we'll just have to starve to death...

... or else be drowned. The wind's rising and the sea's getting rough.

Meanwhile ...

It's hopeless to go on searching. We'll never find them ...

Coffin to port!

Ah, I see it! Lower a boat and rescue the Ancient Mariner!

A few minutes later...

Retrieved one coffin with occupant Sophocles Sarcophagus. Weather worsening. Propose break off search.

As soon as you get a reply to that, bring it to me on the bridge.

O. K. skipper.

Filthy weather! And the glass is still falling. We're in for a real blow!

Signal, captain.

Secure your prisoner. If storm prevents further search abandon two other coffins and proceed to Rendezvous Three.

Good. That's more like it. We're heading south, and none too soon!

We're finished, Snowy!

Ah, he's waking up at last!

Where am I?

Now I remember... We were hit by a gigantic wave... and that was that...

Hello, young Sinbad! How are you?... Slept well?

Yes, but how in the world did I get here?

Just happened to be passing, old boy, when you were going down for the third time!

You saved my life, Captain!

Forget it... But I must admit I'm dying to know what you were doing, floating around the Red Sea in a coffin.

I wish I knew that myself!

Ah, here's my passenger: Senhor Oliveira da Figueira, from Lisbon.

'Morning

Delighted, dear sir, delighted!

Allow me to assist you, sir. Any little thing you may require, sir... and my prices will astonish you...

Just let me show you, sir. Absolutely no obligation. Now observe these exquisite ties...

Beautiful!... Beautiful!... Look how it suits you sir... matches your eyes... Quite, quite perfect...

And what about a sword? Real Toledo steel!

Everything a bargain! An alarm clock? A toothbrush? A biro?

Just as well I didn't fall for his patter. You end up with all sorts of useless junk if you're not careful.

That's the Arabian coast. We're landing there.

You can carry my things over there.

You're setting up shop? ...Here? It's the middle of nowhere. You won't get a single customer!

Wait! I haven't started advertising yet.

Hello! Hello! Salaam Aleikum! Here we are again! Senhor Oliveira da Figueira at your service...

...bringing you the wonders of the western world. Walk up, my friends, walk up, don't be shy... don't miss this marvellous opportunity.

It's the solo supermarket!

Roll up, roll up, lords of the desert. Act today, don't delay! Oliveira da Figueira is waiting to serve you.

What about this hat? Fit for a pharaoh! Make you the best-dressed man in the oasis!

LISBON

This'll be a nice surprise for my wife!

There you are! Clean as a whistle. That's salesman-ship for you! What's more, they all come back, too!

كنّا كي
كي
!

!

Son of a mangy dog! You sold me this cake! I ate it, and now look what's happened!

But... but that's a cake of soap!

Before the new moon rises, by Allah, my master Sheik Patrash Pasha will have you flogged!

Next morning...

Let's explore, Snowy...

He comes!

What a quiet, empty place this is!

Patrash Pasha will be pleased!

Salaam Aleikum, most noble Sheik: the prisoner comes!

Bring him before me!

Aha! So it is you! It is you who tried to poison the servants of Patrash Pasha, infidel dog!

You mind your language!

We can do without the worthless clutter of your so-called civilisation!

What is your name?

My name? It won't mean a thing to you...

...but at home they call me Tintin.

Tintin! Can it be true? ...Allah be praised... Come to my arms!

?

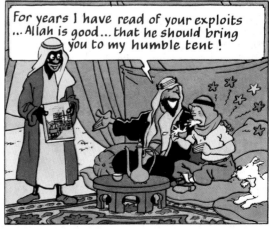

For years I have read of your exploits ...Allah is good...that he should bring you to my humble tent!

Some hours later...

Goodbye, my friend. You have the finest of my horses. May you travel safely.

I will!

Goodbye, Tintin; Allah go with you!

Goodbye, and thank you, noble Sheik!

Amazing what a little publicity will do for you!

Hello? I must be seeing things! A city, here?

HELP!...MERCY!...HELP!...

!

I can hear someone screaming...

HELP!...SAVE ME!...

That's a woman's voice...

MERCY! PITY!...

Brutes!

Don't be afraid... you've seen the last of those ruffians.

Idiot! Imbecile! Silly nitwit!

?

A whole sequence to reshoot, thanks to you!

He's absolutely ruined my entrance!

Oh heavens, I've barged in on a film company!

You deserve to be...

I'm sorry...How could I know...?

What's going on here?

Sir Galahad here has wrecked my scene!

By Lucifer! Unless I'm much mistaken, you're the young man I had that little tiff with aboard the 'Isis'.

Why, it's Mr. Rastapopoulos!

I'm sorry I lost my temper!

And I'm sorry if I messed up your film.

Pah! Think nothing of it! We're making a Superscope-Magnavista feature of "Arabian Knights". We've built a whole city not far from here.

I know. I saw it.

But what are you doing here, all by yourself in the middle of the desert? Come and explain...

Certainly...

An hour later...

...So there you are, Mr. Rastapopoulos. That's my story. Remarkable, isn't it?

Indeed, dear boy. I find it fascinating!

I'm sorry we cannot keep you here, my friend.

You're very kind, but the captain of the dhow will be wondering where I am.

There she is, Snowy. We'll soon be back on board now.

Meanwhile...

Hmm... fresh instructions. We're to forget about Tintin, and look for gun-runners along the Arab coastline.

I can't see a soul on deck.

How odd, all gone... not so much as a whisker...

Sorry, I was wrong. At least puss stayed behind...Here, Snowy!

GRRR

Wooah! Wooah!

Snowy, come here at once!

?

Great snakes! Machine-guns, under an old tarpaulin!

And rifles hidden beneath a layer of umbrellas!

I wonder where that cat went to ...

UMBRELLAS

EXP

...All these crates are packed with ammunition! It's like an arsenal down here!

BEANS

SUGAR

More automatic weapons! What a fool I've been. It didn't cross my mind... this innocent little ship: gun-running!

FRAGILE

Interesting, eh?

?

!

In trouble?... I wonder...

All right, I'll put up my hands...

BANG

BANG

BANG

Lights! Quick! I've got him!

Me too! I'm holding him!

? ?

He must be down here somewhere...We'll soon find him

Not over this side...

Nor here...

We must stop him slipping out...

To be precise: we must stop slipping!

GLUB... GLUB...

?

Did you hear that?

Yes, it sounded quite close...

? ?

GLUB... GLUB

Sorry, I just couldn't stay under water any longer!

Saved!

Lucky for us he hooked himself ...

Hurry up or he'll drown!

You'd better catch that animal while I take care of his master!

Stop, in the name of the law!

It's going to take more than that to catch me!

You're under ar—   rest!

Help! Everybody out!

Help! He's dropped a grenade! We're going   up!

Funny, something must have frightened him...

Panic stations!...Cut the cables! ...We're blowing up!

Goodness gra- cious!...Tintin!

Oh dear, we forgot!

What's up with them? One min- ute they arrest me, the next they bolt like a couple of rabbits.

A pity about Tintin ...

Yes... I say, does a grenade take long to explode ?

Lucky for us they ship gren- ades without explosive ... otherwise we'd be sitting on a cloud by now, Snowy.

The fuse just went "phut".

Come on, Snowy, don't let's hang around here.

We'll head for the Cosmos camp. I'm sure Mr. Rastapopoulos will be able to help us on our way.

There's the camp. I wonder what he will say when I tell him about our latest adventure.

My dear chap, it's exactly like a film. Anyone would think there was a plot to get rid of you!

Next morning...

Good luck!

Goodbye!...And thank you again!

Still no explosion ...

Don't be impatient ...Must be delayed action ...

If all goes well we'll be in Abudin by tomorrow. But we must go easy on the water...

There aren't any wells on our way. And the desert spells death without water.

BANG BANG

Down! Quick! BANG

BANG

BING BLOSH

My water-bottle!

Hoofbeats!... A deliberate attack?...

Yes, that's it: and when he saw he'd failed, whoever it was took to his heels.

He may have missed me, but he hit my water-bottle... and that's nearly as bad.

Many hours later...

An oasis, Snowy! We're in luck!

You see, one should never give up hope!

!

DANGER
MIRAGE AHEAD

Oh Snowy, I'm afraid we rejoiced too soon ...

23

Snowy! Snowy! We're saved!

Look! This time it isn't a mirage!

A drink at last!

Hello, two Bedouin. We'll ask them for some water.

Them!

Him!

Ha!

In the name of the law...

Clever dick! If I hadn't listened to you we wouldn't be wearing these nightshirts... and then we wouldn't have tripped ourselves up!

Smart Aleck! If we hadn't been disguised as Arabs he'd never have thought we were!

We'll soon catch him up ...he was nearly exhausted...

There he is!

Yes, that's him!

WHACK

اكرلا ؟ شنتك !؟ سنع اللن ؟؟ بري بري ؟؟ بي ؟؟

Bother! We were mistaken!

To be precise: we're a mistake.

Come on, Snowy. We mustn't give up.

We're going to need all the courage we've got...To die of thirst...

There... I must be dreaming... palm trees... a town ... I said we mustn't give up...

Water, Snowy, water! Wonderful luck!

And the town... Let's hope this one isn't just a film set!

Hello, what's going on?

What's going on? One of our sheiks was brutally attacked by two men of the Djelababi tribe. It's war!

Crumbs! I've chosen a bad moment to arrive!

Hey, you! Why haven't you reported to the recruiting office?

What for?

What for? I'll give you what for! Me! Corporal Abu-Bin-Dun!

RECRUITING OFFICE

Tough nut, sir! ... Fancies himself! Refused to enlist!

A tough nut, eh? We'll see. You must educate him, corporal!

Left...right...left...right...pick 'em up there, you horrible layabouts!

Halt! Order arms! Enough for to-day. Forty miles route march tomorrow. Squad, dismiss!

A rest at last!

ALI-BHAI!

ALI-BHAI!

Some poor chap in trouble ...

You! Jump to it when I call you! Don't fool with me!

Who, me? I ...

Four days confined to barracks! Now, clean up the colonel's office ... And watch your step!

?

Stupid idiot! How could I forget I gave the name Ali-Bhai when I enlisted?

?

FLOR FINA

Great Snakes! The cigars of the Pharaoh! With the identical band! It's incredible!

Maybe I can find a whole box of them ...

Got one! Hooray!

A spy! Call out the guard!

Get moving, you men! Arrest him! Lock him up!

That's my luck! Just when I was getting to the bottom of the mystery...

Spying...in wartime ...Now I really am in a jam...

...The sentence of the court is that Private Ali-Bhai be shot at dawn...The execution will take place tomorrow... The sentence will be communicated to the prisoner forthwith!

Shot!...I'm going to be shot...My poor, poor Snowy...This is the end!

A note... "Have courage: help is at hand. A Friend." A friend?... Here?...

My last night on earth. Unless...

Tintin!... Tintin!...

?

Who... who are you?

Ssh!...Here's a file. Cut through the bars.

Hurry up! It's nearly dawn...

RRRZ
RRRZ
RRRZ

Done it!

Come, quick!

No time to lose!

Coming!

Free!

HALT!... OR I FIRE!

!

This is the spot... Now to work!

!?

Wooah! Wooah! Wooah!

ALI-BHAI
~SPY~

Quiet! I've come to save your master!

Save my master?

ALI-BHAI
~SPY~

Tintin?... Tintin?... Are you there?

Yes.

?

You've saved my life, madam. I can never...

Come.

Where?

No questions... Follow me.

Here we are.

Come in quickly.

Ladies, I shall never forget what you have done for me. Just before the execution the sergeant told me the rifles would be loaded with blanks. I collapsed when they fired, and pretended to be dead. I did everything he told me, and that saved my life... But who are you?... And why did you rescue me...?

Who are we? Take a good look!

You?!!

Yes, us! We'd have seen you shot over our dead bodies!

But why? Why did you do it?

Simple! We were ordered to arrest Tintin, drug-smuggler and gun-runner, and an order is an order. That's why!

RAT TAT TAT

?

Open! Open quickly! It's the grave-digger!

All is lost! We are betrayed! The soldiers are coming! We shall be slaughtered!

That's it!... Break down the door!

There...look...They've escaped across the roof!

Yes, and they've taken the ladder!

Down the street! We'll catch them!

Whew...they've gone ... Now then...

Off we go! There isn't a moment to lose!

Shuddering sheiks! It's the dead spy! Sound the alarm!

Treason!... Murder!... Kill him!

A plane! ... If I could only ... No, there's a guard ...

It's my only chance... I must try ... Help! ... Help!

Help! Help! Save me! The dog... It's gone mad ... stop it!...

Who?... Me?

It worked! He's bolted! We're free!

?

That's a very old trick, Snowy ... Go into a spin, then disappear into the clouds. But our troubles aren't over, by any means... We're running low on fuel.

!

Not a hope of landing in that jungle ...

...and no sign of a clearing ... How much longer ...

That's it! The engine's stopped... Out of juice ...

Hold tight, Snowy! ... Here we go!

CRACK

The first aid kit! All I need is a book of instructions!

HOME DOCTOR

Any more to come?

Now, I wonder where we are. Somewhere in India, I'm sure, but impossible to tell exactly.

!

Don't be afraid, old chap. Snowy wouldn't hurt a fly.

Wooah! Wooah!

Good heavens, you're ill. You're running a temperature ... Wait, I've just the thing for you.

What he needs is a good dose of quinine ...

A whole tube! That should be enough.

There, swallow that.

A lightning cure!

Hey! Take it easy, old man!

Put me down ... at once!

Where in the world is he taking me?

?

Look, brother elephants, this young human has cured my fever.

They seem to be having a conference. Now I can slip away.

Hrrrrm! Hrrrrm! Stop, little human. You must stay with us... You are our elephant doctor.

Some days later...

You see, Snowy, when the elephants talk to one another they make a sort of trumpeting sound. I've been listening to them...

I think I may be able to pick up some of their language. Perhaps I can discover what they're saying, and even talk to them. All I need is a trumpet. So that's what I'm making.

It isn't all that difficult. SOL-LAH-TE-DOH means 'yes'. DOH-TE-LAH-SOL means 'no'. 'I want a drink' goes SOL-SOL-FAH-FAH... Of course the main problem is to get a good accent..

Phew! I'm hot! ... I wonder... Why don't I try...

♪ ♪♪♪♪♪

Did he understand?

He did! He's coming back! Hooray, I've learnt to talk Elephant!

Now you stay here. I'm going for a walk.

It's time I did a bit of exploring.

!

Kih-Oskh! The symbol, here!... It's unbelievable!!

Who on earth could have painted that sign?

The ♪Sheik♪ of ♪Araby♪🎵

It can't be!

Doctor Sarcophagus!

Doctor! Hello! How in the world did you get here?

Tell me what happened ... everything, since you floated away in the coffin ...

Ssh! Not so loud!

I'll tell you. But you must promise to keep it a secret.

Of course... Now then ...

Well, absolutely between ourselves, I'm the Pharaoh Rameses II!

Tweet, tweet!... Don't tell a soul ... Nobody knows... I'm travelling incognito.

Poor Doctor Sarcophagus... He's completely mad. I shan't get anything out of him until he's cured. But where can I find a doctor?

Where?... Of course! That's easy!

I used to play the piano too when I was a boy...

What does the little human want of me?

Good day, my dear Tutankhamen.

We need special help... Can you take us to a village?

Look!... A bungalow!

Good morning. I hope we aren't disturbing you...

?

I found this man wandering in the jungle. He seems to have gone out of his mind. Is there a doctor anywhere near?

You're in luck. Dr. Finney is up visiting this area. I'll send for him right away.

Look!... There!... Our sign!!

That's the whole story, doctor. Do you think the poor fellow might be cured one day?

Yes, he could... but he needs treatment as soon as possible. There's a special hospital not far from here; the superintendent is a friend of mine. You could take him there in the morning.

Meanwhile, you're my guest. I've just fixed a small party for tonight: do join us.

Later... Tintin... Our good padre the Reverend Peacock...

... Mr. and Mrs. Snowball...

... the well-known poet, Zloty.

That's a strange weapon you have there. Isn't it a Hindu dagger?

Yes, a kukri...

It's made of steel... a deadly little toy!... I was given it by a fakir. He told me it had magic powers... It's supposed to point to anyone whose life is in danger.

I'll get it down for you to see...

!

OH!!!

I'm so sorry. I do hope you won't take it as a bad omen.

Please don't worry. It's just a coincidence... Anyway, I'm not scared of omens!

BANG

CENTURY JR. HIGH SCHOOL

Next morning...

The young sahib went out at dawn, into the forest.

Try not to lose the trail, Snowy...

Look!...There's his hat!

Yes, it's certainly his. We're on the right track ...He's somewhere around.

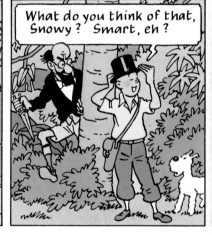

What do you think of that, Snowy? Smart, eh?

Help! he's gone berserk! ... Run for it!

Lucky his arm got tangled in the creeper. Otherwise ...

40

So! You cannot resist me!

Ooh, pretty little peashooter!

Whoopee! What a jolly game! Ram-Ram's playing bang-bang!

I'll shoot you, naughty thing!

BANG BANG

Whew! Thank goodness! ...Just a butterfly.

Bang-bang all gone.

Never mind, let's go.

The fakir managed to escape... No use going after him... Let's concentrate on the poet... He can only mean that Zloty fellow.

A few minutes later...

Let's have the cards on the table, Mr. Zloty. Someone's trying to murder me. And you're going to tell me precisely what you know about it...

Me?... But I don't understand...

You're lying! Talk, and talk fast!

Or else... bang!

Wait!...I...yes ...I...

I don't know very much... There's an international gang of drug smugglers...They're determined to get rid of you ...

And you're a member of the gang?

Yes...No...I mean...There is a branch of the organisation here... You were recognised and someone reported to the boss...

And who is the boss?

Just a minute... The boss was furious that you were still alive: he gave orders for you to be liquidated... Sarcophagus was to do it, while he was hypnotised...

But the boss... Tell me his name!

No... I can't... it's impossible... They are merciless to traitors... it's horrible...

You're going to tell me, now!

I...he...his name is ...

Someone was hiding outside the shutters...

Too late... I'm done for... It's their revenge... This arrow is poisoned with Rajaijah juice, the poison of madness.

The boss ...film ...don't trust...

Quick! Quick!

Here we come ♫ gathering ♫ ♭♭ nuts in May ... ♪

Come along, children, playtime is over now...

Who can tell me who succeeded Rameses II?

Me, sir... Napoleon.

Later . . .

Now we've got two madmen on our hands.

We'll send them to hospital tomorrow.

Next morning . . .

Here's a letter for the superintendent.

Ha! ha! Off to hospital, my clever friend. With that letter they'll certainly give you a warm welcome!

Here's a letter from Dr. Finney about these two patients.

Hmm... Yes... I see... Quite so...

Orderly, look after these gentlemen, please.

Will you come with me? ... Just a few formalities ...

Certainly.

There's nothing to be afraid of. They're quite harmless.

This is the sort of ward we shall use for treating your poor friends.

SLAM

?

"He will give you this letter himself. He will tell you it concerns his two companions..."

"...He is extremely dangerous. You should trick him into entering a cell, rather than force him. He will keep on insisting that he is absolutely sane..."

So, gentlemen, your unhappy friend will have all possible care.

We have complete confidence in you.

Goodbye, gentlemen.

Happy birthday, nanny!

Hello... yes boss. I copied the doctor's writing, and substituted another letter... It made out that Tintin himself was mad, not the others, and ...

WOOAH! WOOAH!

THUMP THUMP THUMP THUMP

THUMP THUMP THUMP THUMP

If you don't keep quiet we'll put you in a strait-jacket! Understand?

If this is some sort of game, doctor, it's time it stopped. It isn't me that's mad, it's the other two I brought here...

Just as Doctor Finney said: "He will keep on insisting that he is absolutely sane."

Mad? They think I'm mad? It's unbelievable!

Here is your soup.

My soup?

Are you joking?

That's what I think of your soup!

?

Ye-o-o-ow!... Ye-o-o-w!

This is it! Now or never...

Help! Help!

Just the wall, and I'm free!

Crikey! How can I get over that?!

?

46

Oh no! My escape ... cut off!

I'll have to jump for it: If I stop I'm done for! Here goes ...

Hey, wait for me!

Confound it! He's escaped!

Wooah! Wooah!

Safe at last! Let's hope Snowy follows the railway track. I'll hop off as soon as I can.

Well, well, what a surprise to see your face again! We'd lost you completely!

To be precise: we'd completely lost face!

Tintin! Now I shall never see him again ...

? ? ?

I've got him!

Me too!

Goodness gracious! It's the ticket collector!

To be precise: we've collected a ticket!

He can't have gone too far.

No, we aren't too far gone.

Hello? Jamjah... the station? One of our patients has escaped, jumped aboard a train heading in your direction. I'll describe him for you...

An hour later...

How can I get off the platform without a ticket? ...

No mistake, it's him all right... Matches the description exactly...

What do they want with me?

Crumbs! Now I understand... My escape has been reported...

Hey, you! Stop!

STOP!...

Lucky for me I bought some bananas!

One ...

Two ...

Just wait, cleverdick ... We'll pay you back!

WAY OUT

And that's for number three ...

ZZIP

All that, just to end up in a strait-jacket. Poor Snowy, if you could see your master now!

Meanwhile ...

O Siva-the-destroyer, graciously accept the sacrifice I am about to offer.

The superintendent will be pleased to recover ...

...this awkward customer!

...The patient! Where's he gone?

Quick! Look around! He can't be far away.

Free! ... I'm free!...

Meanwhile...

Die, infidel dog!

Stay your hand, servant of Siva! The god will not accept so mean a sacrifice!

He's gone: it's all clear.

To be precise: the all clear's gone!

Quick ... untie him.

How wrong I was. They're really pretty good chaps!

Ha ha! If we follow the dog we'll find the master.

And in the jungle...

By the holy brahmin! Look, Highness, look!

By Siva!... That music!

No one! No one at all... Not a sign...

It's horrible...I must tell you... My father and my brother both went mad, one after the other. Each time, just before they became ill, the same unearthly music was heard outside the palace...

This time I am sure it is for me... It is a warning...

...Rajaijah, the poison of madness...

Maharaja, when your father and your brother went mad, was there any sign of a wound, a puncture, on the neck or arm?

No, nothing...why?

Were they perhaps trying to fight the traffic in narcotics? Opium, for instance?

Indeed they were. And I am continuing their struggle. The poppy from which opium is made flourishes in this region. The drug traffickers terrorise my people. They force the peasants to grow poppies instead of food, and purchase..

...the crop for a miserable sum. Then, when the unhappy people need the rice they should have grown for themselves, they have to buy it from the smugglers at exorbitant prices. I never stop fighting the devilish organisation.

Good. We will work together. Listen carefully, Highness...

That night...

You see?...There... That window in the middle...

Magic rope, obey your master!

52

Aha! It is done...There goes the last of our mad maharajas!

Careful... he's coming...

What the...?!

Hey, where can he have gone?

Is he hiding in the tree?

...In the tree!?

Oho, that sounds hollow...

BOM
BOM
BOM

The problem is to find out how it opens...

Got it!

A well!

Strange...?!

Where does this lead to?

A door...

Careful! Someone's coming...

Crumbs! Another one!...
No time to lose!

OW!

BUMP
WHACK
THUMP

Right!

RAT TAT TAT

Brothers, with the exception of our leader, who is unable to come, we are all present. Our session may begin. Our brother from the West will speak first.

I have the best possible news for the Brotherhood: We are finally rid of the Maharaja of Gaipajama. Even as I speak, he is going mad!

There is nothing now to prevent...

RRRING
RRRING
RRRING

Hello?... Yes, headquarters here ...A message from Cairo?...What?!... Hold the line a moment.

Brothers, things look black. Our Cairo hideout has been raided. Only our leader escaped. He's on his way here   by air...

Hello?... What?... Someone's just found what?...One of the brothers?!... But...but there are seven of us here...

BROTHERS, WE HAVE A SPY IN OUR MIDST!

?   ?

Since our rules forbid us to uncover our faces, you will come one by one and give me our password. Whoever fails to give the word dies instantly!

....

Good... Next!

....

Right... Next!

I... I'm sorry... but I... I can't remember... I...

HAHA!

I will count up to three, my friend. If by that time you haven't given the password, I fire!

But... I... Er...

ONE!

TWO!

Wait! Wait! I've got it! I remember! KIH-OSKH and GAIPAJAMA!

!

Stupid fool! You're supposed to whisper! Now everybody knows!

Never mind! I am going into the next room. You will come in one by one and give me the password for our last meet-ing.

First!

Next!

Next!

Last one!

THWACK

Not a bad day's work!... I must say I was lucky to be called first... Now, let's have a look at the faces of our jungle Ku Klux Klan!

The fakir, a Japanese, Mr. and Mrs. Snowball, the colonel who sentenced me to death, and the Maharaja's secretary ... It's fantastic!

?

Tintin!... Him!! ...Here!!!

What a cheek, thinking he could tie me up... Me, a fully qualified fakir!

The fakir! He's escaped!

CLACK

Great snakes! I mustn't let him get away!

BANG

Aha! Now I really have you in my power!

YOWK !

YEEEEK!

?

Hands up!

Snowy!!

Congratulations, my friend, you've brought off a masterly coup!

Hey! Don't you want to arrest me any more?

Certainly not. We know you are innocent. We had a call from the Cairo police. They found a gang of international drug-smugglers using the tomb of the Pharaoh Kih-Oskh. It was their secret hideout ...

Among the papers they seized was a list of their enemies. It included you, and the Maharaja of Gaipajama. And there was a plan of this bolt-hole, too. We heard about it, so this is where we are.

To be precise: so where are we?

As for me, Tintin, I owe you my life. The dummy you put in my bed was hit by the arrow... the arrow intended for me.

CLACK

!

The fakir! He's given us the slip again!

Wretched fellow! He's locked us in!

Wait, I have a skeleton.

By the time we get the door open he'll be miles away. No use chasing after him. We can pick him up later on. Let's go back to the palace, and send someone to look after the rest of the prisoners.

A few minutes later...

Highness! Highness! The crown prince, your son! He's been kidnapped! Two men, they made off in a car ...

Quick, the garage. They haven't got much of a start ...

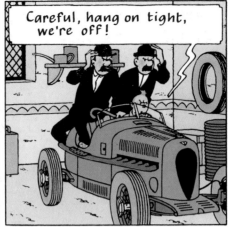

Careful, hang on tight, we're off!

VROOM

Don't fall off, you two! This is going to be rough!

There they are!

We are pursued, O Master! ... Hurry!

The car won't go any faster.

We're gaining ground!

Smoke! What's happened?

Oh, the poor devils!

They must have skidded on the corner ...

As soon as he climbs down to have a look we jump in his car and get going!

Supposing it's a trap ... I just wonder ...

Lucifer! He isn't going down. He'll go back to the palace, and we'll have no car ... We'll soon stop that!

BANG

Gangsters! A good thing I wasn't fooled!

Impossible to get him. You keep him occupied while I make a break with the kid.

Now where is he? I can't see...

Hands up, Houdini! And drop your gun!

There, that's better. Just a minor detail, but my gun wasn't loaded.

What a coincidence! My gun happens to be empty too. So it's just the two of us...

I couldn't have done it better myself!

While Snowy guards the fakir, I'll go after the mystery man...

Diavolo! Can I never be rid of him?... But wait...

Come along, dear boy, just a little bit nearer...

HELP!!

... Missed! But I'm not finished yet ...

CRACK

Poor wretch. Who was he? ... I wonder if we shall ever know... or has he taken his secret with him?

Ah, there's the prince. I must get him back to the palace.

A little later...

My son!

Daddy!

Now, if your Highness will excuse me, I must say goodbye and start on my long journey home.

No, no, Tintin, I don't want you to go!

Allow me to insist, Tintin. You must stay for a few days at least.

Thank you, your Highness. I shall be delighted.

Hip hip hooray!

DRUG GANG SMASHED

...MOS KING ...NISHES

...AIRO, Monday ...ion grows here ...e fate of millionaire ...agnate Rasta-...s, reported missing ...ay from his desert ...mp. No news has ...ceived since his un-...ned departure in his ...e plane for an un-...n destination. Search ...s have been operating ...dawn in desert areas ...e west.

ROYAL HOSTAGE FREED

Reporter Tintin cracked the final link in an international drug-smuggling chain, and following a dramatic mountain chase the boy Crown Prince of Gaipajama, held hostage by the gang leader, was freed. The narcotics boss, whose identity is still a mystery, plunged to his death down a precipice. ...dy has not yet been ...earch

...MOON SHOT

An informal shot of Messrs. Thomson and Thom...son, detectives in the drug case, answering an urge... call to headquarters.

A few days later...

Long live Rameses II !

! !

Play up! Play up! Now! Pass to the wing!

Hooray for Tutankhamen!

A goal! A goal!... Magnificent shot!

Highness, could you arrange for those two men to be brought to the palace. They need help...

And later that day...

Greetings, most noble Pharaoh!

They're still quite mad...

Bring cigars and a drink for our guests.

Stop! Remember, it is forbidden to touch the cigars of the Pharaoh!

?

Tell me quickly, where did you find these cigars?

They belonged to the Maharaja's former secretary. I knew he kept these hidden away. So when I couldn't find any of our usual brand, I brought these.

Just as I thought...The identical cigars! We found them in the tomb of Kih-Oskh... And the Arab colonel had some. Now let me see...

As I expected, they're fakes. The band, an outer covering of tobacco, and inside, opium! Quite a simple trick, but it fooled the police of half the world.

Well done, Tintin!...But what about our friends here?

The Rolls? Thank you, my man.

The gentlemen's conveyance is waiting.

They will be well cared for... And you, my young friend, have earned a good holiday. Maybe a nice quiet cruise... now that we have seen the last of that evil gang.

I hope you are right, Highness, I certainly hope so... But somehow, I wonder...

HERGÉ.

THE END